WARNING

This book contains sexually explicit scenes and adult language. It may be considered offensive to some readers. This book is for sale to adults ONLY.

* * * * * * * * * * * * * * * * * *

Please store your files wisely where they cannot be accessed by underage readers.

ISBN-13: 978-1987863208
ISBN-10: 1987863208

Other Books by Darla Dunbar:

<u>The Romeo Alpha BBW Paranormal Shifter Romance Series</u>

Amanda Walker thinks that she has a normal and boring life. That is until after her 24th birthday. Everything changes when she meets the man who says he was supposed to be her husband. Denying everything the man says, she fights him every step of the way. But after he kidnaps her, Amanda discovers that there are some things about her family that her parents kept a secret all these years. Among the history of the family she learns secrets she thought only happened in story books. Can Amanda tell the difference between truth and lies or is she this mysterious woman that holds the key to a legacy?

<u>Romeo Alpha Blood Lines Romance Series</u>

Twenty-four years have passed in relative peace for Amanda and Romeo. They've raised five children into adulthood and are thoroughly enjoying their lives as the Alpha King and Queen of the werewolves. At twenty-four, Sarina is just stepping into her powers and will be ripe for mating when her birthday comes in two weeks. What no one knows is the danger that lurks just outside their tight knit community. Romeo has made peace with the other clans and has enjoyed that peace, but it will all come crashing down around him when his oldest daughter comes of age to take a mate.

The Alpha Feud BBW Paranormal Shifter Romance Series

Eliza's life consisted of reporting on boring, crowd-pleasing events, like their country livestock fair. With the arrival of two handsome brothers, the lives of Eliza and her best friend, Melissa, are shaken to the core. For Eliza, the arrival of this new man becomes a test of her relationship with her current boyfriend, who she's been happily living with for over six years. Does Hayden, a complete stranger, really wield the power to make Eliza reconsider her relationship with Andrew?

The Alpha Packed BBW Paranormal Shifter Romance Series

Darlene has led a quiet life since suffering through a terrible break-up. She wants nothing more than to spend her time in front of the TV, away from any sort of trouble. But all that goes down the drain when handsome, rugged and rough Idris comes into her life. He is a werewolf on the lookout for his missing pack leader. Darlene quickly finds herself pulled towards this mysterious man and at the same time finds herself falling deeper and deeper into the world of the supernatural.

The Mind Talker Paranormal Romance Series

Ananda finds herself on the run and she's not alone. With help from Jared, a stranger that she just met, the two evade capture by an organization that is intent on hunting her kind. Ananda and Jared are able to read minds. When an unfortunate incident happened involving a disturbed individual that resulted in the death of his schoolmates, the secret organization decided to take action.

<u>The Leather Satchel Paranormal Romance Series</u>

Valtina is stuck in Middle World, unable to pass on to The Afterlife. In order to redeem herself from past deeds done, she must help bring romance back into the world and stop The Dark Side from destroying love in its entirety. Following orders issued by Ladaya and armed with a leather satchel filled with the appropriate tools and weapons, Valtina embraces each mission with enthusiasm.

Get the latest update on new releases from the author at:

https://darladunbar.com/newsletter/

This book is Part Seven of "<u>The Daemon Paranormal Romance Chronicles</u>"

Book 1 - The Awakening

Phoebe grew up not knowing her mother. The stranger, Apollo Mikos, claimed to know her mother. After that day, Phoebe's life would change forever.

Book 2 - The Shifter

Phoebe is surprised when her dog, Ace, shows up from nowhere. She is on a mission with Apollo to kill the Qilin. That is the only way that the true leader of daemons will emerge.

Book 3 - Forgotten

Juno has been stirring up trouble that has prolonged the infighting among the daemons. In order to get her to stop, Phoebe agrees to give up a year of her memories. But making deals with a siren is never a good thing. Without her memories, Phoebe's romantic relationship with Supay no longer exists. Instead, she leaves Supay for Apollo.

Book 4 - The Siren's Trap

The unsuspecting couple, Phoebe and Supay, made a deal with Juno to stop the infighting among the daemons. But at what price? An entire year was wiped clean from Phoebe's mind. Now Phoebe was with Apollo. Desperate to get her back, Supay considers Juno's new deal. Is it worth the price to pay for the dubious result? To win back Phoebe's love, Supay will need to be unfaithful to her.

Book 5 - Exposed

Hiding away in Peru, Supay and Phoebe start their own family, away from the chaos and the daemon infighting. Meanwhile, Apollo, heart-broken and lost, is lured into another one of Juno's schemes. Making deals with a siren never turns out right. If Apollo accepts the deal, the love of his life may resent him for the rest of his natural life. If he doesn't take the deal, she is lost to him forever.

Book 6 - The Beginning

As preparations for the war between daemons are underway, everyone must begin to choose. Siding temporarily with Apollo, Juno has a moment to look back on her life and figure out how she arrived at this moment. As she sifts through memories of the past, a specific dark stranger stands out. How far will young Juno go with her new love? More importantly, will her mother, Circe, discover the secret tryst?

Book 7 - The Treachery

Having broken the cardinal rule of the sirens, Juno must take action to save her own life and the life of her unborn child. In order to keep her secret safe from the sisterhood, she must kill her lover and conceal her shame. Will Juno betray the sisterhood and save her lover or will she remain loyal by slaying him instead?

Book 8 - Duplicity

Juno's mother, Circe, discovers her lies and gives her an ultimatum to fix everything. As Juno races against the clock to protect her loved ones from Circe, she makes a final choice that could leave her perpetually unhappy. Left to wander the world alone, Juno realizes that freedom means nothing if there is no one to share it with. The nature of Juno's vendetta—and the means she achieves it with—are finally revealed.

Book 9 - Reconnaissance

As Juno's hunt for the daemon's fortress unfolds, Apollo is left alone wondering if she will truly return to him. Will Juno be able to resist her base instincts? More importantly, will she be able to get to the fortress and return without being spotted? Discover how Juno's stealth mission works out.

Book 10 - The Interrogation

Juno tries to hide her rising fear in the presence of her captors. As her fear mounts, she holds on to the hope that Phoebe or Supay will take pity on her. Before that can happen, she has to come clean to Supay about her past. Could he possibly forgive her for what she has done? Will Juno remain faithful to Apollo or will her siren urges take over? Discover how the confrontation with Supay unfolds.

The Daemon Paranormal Romance Chronicles

The Treachery

Book Seven

By Darla Dunbar

Copyright Revelry Publishing 2015

Table of Contents

Chapter One...1
Chapter Two...6
Chapter Three...9
Chapter Four...18
Other Books by Darla Dunbar............................31
About the Author - Darla Dunbar 32
Connect with Darla Dunbar.................................33

Chapter One

THE SOUND of footsteps jarred Juno out of the darkness of her memories. With her mind refocused, she realized she was back within the castle in Sicily. She gazed around, confused and tried to spot the source of the interruption. Amid the gloomy shadows of the tower door stood Apollo. Juno hid the confusion and annoyance on her face.

Juno needed to fix her mess before she could walk over to Apollo. Moments prior, she used the scrying bowl to review images of her past. Now, she acted to hide any evidence. Although her memories were not confidential in any way, she did not want him to see some of her most painful recollections. She pulled a pinch of sand from her pouch and sprinkled it over the magical bowl. With a wave of her hand, she whispered, "*Finite.*" The replay of her past disappeared from the surface of the water.

With her most seductive face, Juno slinked toward Apollo, sexier than the best of sirens. "What brings you here, my darling? Weren't you preparing the archers?" Juno circled his figure and leaned in to run her teeth down the edge of his ear. Biting lightly, she pulled away.

It did not matter how much time he and Juno spent together. Her scent still affected him in an intoxicating way. A hint of jasmine washed over his senses; he struggled to keep his face from responding to her physicality. Juno was more than a woman to him. She was a temptation and the physical embodiment of sensuality. He may be repulsed by her actions, but he could not control himself when he was around her body. Apollo tried to act nonchalant as he steadied his voice. "There's no point in helping the archers. They are positioned on the wrong side of the castle. Invaders will be able to surmount the wall with little effort while the boiling tar is placed above a wall that is too high for it to ever be needed."

Juno smiled. A few hours earlier, she was thinking the same thought. Perhaps Apollo was smarter than he appeared. "I agree. What brings you to my lonely tower, my sweet?" She smiled. Even in the darkness, Juno saw Apollo watching her figure with hunger in his eyes. With slow deliberate strides, she allowed her hips to sway hypnotically. In one fluid motion, she sat down upon the settee. In a nonchalant manner, she shifted her skirt from her legs so Apollo could see the full length of her calves and thighs.

Apollo skulked toward her, feeling like the entire world stopped revolving around the poles. In its place, the new pole shifted to this very room. Nothing changed or moved in the tower while life revolved at its own pace in the world outside. In his chest, his heart beat ever faster as he cursed his lack of control. Before him sat the last woman he wanted to be with, but the only person he was physically mated to. He wondered absentmindedly what Juno did before he arrived. He opened his mouth to ask, but forgot his question as he caught her scent again. He gazed down her full body. "I... wanted to see you again," he said.

Those words gave Juno much pleasure. "Well, here I am." She leaned back along the couch and ran her fingers down the side of her neck. At the center of her bosom, she pulled on two strings that held her peasant blouse together. Her outer garment fell open to reveal a dark purple camisole that attempted to hide her nipples beneath them.

Unable to resist any longer, Apollo spread his legs across her body and pinned her to the settee. Without waiting to ask, he ripped her shirt into two pieces with one hand. Her camisole still hid her breasts from his view. Apollo glanced up at Juno as he reached for the straps of the camisole. He pushed the straps down her shoulders and allowed her breasts to break free from the constraints of clothing.

Apollo glanced up at her face and caught a fleeting glance that unnerved him. Unguarded for a brief second in time, her glance appeared almost loving or caring. Before the exact nature of her expression registered itself in his mind, Juno smiled and the moment evaporated. While ignoring this thought for the moment, Apollo lowered his head to her breast and began to lick her nipples. Her round, firm breasts were malleable beneath his giant hands. Ravenous and unsatisfied, Apollo knew he needed her. He also knew he would never stop needing her like this. Each curve of her body tempted him into a never-ending game of seduction.

Beneath his fondling, Juno moaned. Distracted by her memories, she did not realize how much she needed him until this moment. Her legs spread, she forced him between her thighs. With her skirt pulled up, he caught sight of the gentle slope of her thighs and the soft mound between that welcomed him. He could no longer hold back. His head tingled with anticipation as it delved into her wetness. A low guttural moan escaped from within as he thrust his entire shaft into her.

Juno arched her back as she received the satisfaction she needed. Slight whimpers of desire rose from her lips as she urged him on. Her legs wrapped tightly around his form, she pushed her hips against his. The rocking and insatiable desire that emanated from her body only turned Apollo on more. He needed this. If this moment lasted forever, it would be his version of heaven. He thrust into her body deeper; she moaned and dug her nails deeply into his back. The sudden pain served as a catalyst for him and brought him closer to orgasm. Beneath his body, Juno's body started to clench as orgasm approached. With their urges taking over, the couple came as one in a fit of ecstasy. In her mind, Juno floated away from the memories, the doubts and the stresses of the day. The only thing that existed was the body of Apollo and the sensation of him inside of her.

Juno moved Apollo's body off hers as the bright, vivid sensation of orgasm waned from her mind. His spent figure draped like a Greek god across the settee. Juno stepped away to admire Apollo's form. Long, lean muscles stretched taut across his chest and arms. His golden hair was tousled from their recent exertion and his weary eyes followed Juno. The daily preparations for the daemon war took their toll on him. Juno smiled at him. In the last few months, she grew close to Apollo. Without realizing it, she even started developing feelings for him. She tried to hide it, but her emotions remained. With a sigh, Juno turned away. For sirens, having feelings was never a good idea. Without thinking about it, she rubbed the tip of her nipple as she stood above him. Only her skirt remained on. Her shirt was ruined, but it did not bother her. She would take Apollo's button-up shirt later.

Juno looked back at Apollo. He would be asleep in a few moments, but she did not feel like waiting. She slid her fingers over his eyelids and muttered a quiet incantation. In seconds, Apollo fell asleep.

Juno wandered over to the scrying basin again and waved her hand across the surface of the water. In moments, the memories of her past appeared.

Chapter Two

Her mother, Circe, sat in front of Juno. The cold anger in her eyes remained barely hidden as she demanded the name of her lover. Young Juno winced. She may be naive, but she never doubted her mother's ability to kill. Death would be the least terrible thing a full-fledged siren could do to Supay. Juno tried to think about what to do as her mother coolly asked for the man's name again.

Uncertain about what to say, Juno blurted out the first name that came to mind that was not Supay's. "His name is Yossele. He's a golem."

Circe raised an eyebrow. "This child will be half-golem. You... were... with... a... golem." Each word sounded forced as it escaped from her lips. Her anger assaulted Juno from across the table. With a wince, Juno tried to shift away from Circe.

"Mother, what do you mean? What child?" Fear started to grow in the pit of her stomach as she realized the truth of her mother's words. What she was too naive and innocent to see was true. She must be pregnant. The sudden realization she was with child brought about a new realization. Her mother would never forgive her.

Circe stood up and gripped the sides of the table so tight that her knuckles turned white. "You are a blathering idiot and a disgrace to sirens. What did you think would happen? Didn't I tell you to stay away from men until you were old enough to control your siren urges?"

"But mother, it isn't urges I can't control. I love Su... Yossele," said Juno, shrugging.

Circe shook her head. "Sirens do not feel love. We have desires... we enjoy the control and we take pleasure in seducing an unsuspecting man. We do not feel love for a man. Only our sisters are worthy of such a sentiment."

After taking several deep breaths, Circe tried to control her anger. "This disgrace will be fixed. If you plan on the child remaining alive, we will kill the father. No sirens will know of your mistake and you will tell no one about this. Where is the father now?"

Juno's eyes widened. "Kill…?"

Circe nodded. "Did you not think through the repercussions of your actions? Of course, something will happen to Yossele. No one can discover that you broke the cardinal commandments. You better hope this child is ready for birth before siren training starts. If I have to, I will cut it out of you before training so that no one knows your secret."

Juno swallowed and tried to think fast. There had to be a way out. "Mother, it is okay. It was my mistake and I will fix it. Consider the father killed... the child will be born as you wish." She refrained from saying anything else. With her mother's well-known fury and the rules of the sirens, Juno would be lucky if she escaped this situation with her own life and the life of her child. Without thinking about it, she rubbed her belly. Until today, she did not know her womb held a child. What an unusual idea.

Circe nodded. "You will take care of this and I will check. If this is not done to my satisfaction--or if you exhibit your weak ideals about love--your lover will not be the only person who dies."

Chapter Three

In the darkness, Juno peered around the corner. She asked her mother for an incantation to hide her swelling abdomen before leaving. In front of her, was the family farm of Supay. From their many talks, Juno knew she would find him in the loft of the barn. He was beginning to exit adolescence so he still shape shifted every so often during his sleep. Although he mostly transformed between his preferred dog and human forms, he had occasionally woken up as a horse or an elephant. Until his control was greater, he would remain in the barn at night.

Juno was pleased that no one heard her while tiptoeing into barn. The task she had before her was a difficult one, but she could handle it. For her life, Supay's and her child's, she would have to handle a difficult and traumatic task. She saw the sleeping figure of a black dog after rounding a corner. The dog's keen hearing and sense of smell picked up her presence as she approached. In seconds, Supay shifted back into his human form.

Still half asleep and smiling, he opened his arms for her. Juno let out a sigh of relief. Her mother's incantation had successfully hid their unborn child. After rushing forward, she spread her legs across his strong waist and let herself be encapsulated by his embrace. For a few moments, everything was normal again.

Supay held her close and ran his hand along the ivory white of her back. A sudden thought occurred to him as desire started to intermingle with his drowsiness. "Juno," he asked. "What's wrong? I thought we agreed to never meet here. We weren't supposed to meet until I come home from the mines in another month."

Juno shook her head and pouted. The next few hours would take all her acting skills as a siren. "*Mi amor*, I cannot stand being without you for long." She ran her hand down the front of his body and stopped upon his cock. It was hard in expectation. Supay did not stop to ask any more questions but groaned in pleasure instead. It had been months since they had been together and he would no longer wait. He pulled her body down on top of his and entered her in one fluid motion. Surrounded by her pleasing moistness, he groaned again. It was impossible to last any longer.

Above him, Juno rocked in anticipation. The task she had before her tonight did not prevent her from desiring his body. For a siren, unending desire was a fact of life. She moved her hips faster in time with his. Over and over, their hips met together until they orgasmed. Juno cried out in pleasure and fell across his body. "I love you," she said without thinking. Beneath her, Supay turned his head for a kiss.

"I love you too, darling," he whispered. Juno winced and started to run her hands along his body. She had not intended to reaffirm her love. She rubbed her hands along the muscles of his arms in a way only a siren was able to. The hypnotic movements brought Supay back to a drowsy state of mind. Within five minutes, he was asleep again.

Cautiously, Juno pulled her body off his and began to tiptoe around the area. In the corner, she found his jacket. Inside, he still had the words for controlling Yossele. She sighed as she glanced back at Supay. It was going to be better this way. She grabbed her shirt from the floor and began buttoning it as she walked toward the house. From Supay's stories, Juno guessed Yossele would be in one of the top corners of the farmhouse before her. It was time to put her plan into action. Juno took a deep breath and glanced back at the barn. This would most likely be the last time she would ever be with Supay in a romantic sense.

Juno dismissed any doubts from her mind and began to tiptoe into the farmhouse. Around her, the dark halls were filled with silence and random pieces of furniture. A slight creak of the step underneath her foot reminded Juno that her shoes were still on. Ever so silently, she slipped the shoes off and placed them at the bottom of the staircase leading to the second floor. Cloaked in darkness, she managed to make her way up the stairs without making another sound. After peeking into a guest room and the empty master bedroom, she approached the corner she assumed would be Yossele's bedroom. She opened the door and stepped into the room. In front of her, the humongous body of Yossele was sprawled across the bed.

Juno raised the slip of paper toward the moonlight and struggled to say the words. Written in some unknown tongue, the words flowed weirdly across her tongue. She finished the sentence and looked back at Yossele. "I command you, get up," she whispered. Nothing happened. She must have said the phrase incorrectly.

With annoyance in her eyes, she turned back to the window. Being a golem meant that Yossele could be brought under her power. It would only work if she said the correct words. She growled under her breath in anger. Her plan was falling apart. Juno jumped in surprise as she turned back toward the bed. Yossele was staring at her. His large brown eyes and features were so similar to Supay's, but something was off. Instead of the rogue-like dark skin of Supay, he had a cracked clay-like texture to his brownish-gray skin tone. It dawned on her in an instant why they appeared so similar, yet so different. One of the men was from a different mother. Surprisingly, Supay had never mentioned this detail to her.

As she tried to think of something to do or say—or a way to escape—Yossele motioned to her. "Come," he whispered huskily. She crossed the room and perched upon the edge of the bed. Uncertain about what to do, she remained motionless. Next to her, Yossele ran his fingers through her glossy black hair. He smiled and she saw that sleep was quickly leaving his eyes. "You're beautiful. I've never had a dream seem so real before."

The vivid white of Juno's teeth flashed as she bit her plump red lip. He thought she was a dream. Perhaps there was hope for this situation yet. Thanking whatever goddess was watching over her tonight, she pulled herself together and smiled seductively. "I suppose this would be called a lucid dream, my love." Juno leaned forward to run her lips along the curve of his neck. Beneath her, Yossele shivered in pleasure.

Juno closed her eyes. She couldn't do this. Bits of her soul flaked away as she leaned in to kiss Yossele. He was not Supay and she did not love him. Although she needed his help for the plan, this betrayal cut deep into her soul.

Yossele sensed her hesitation and pulled back in confusion. "What's wrong?" he asked.

She realized that she was about to lose her only chance at saving Supay and her child. Juno shook her head and said, "Nothing's wrong, dear Yossele. Lean back and let me pleasure you." Juno pushed him back with the tips of her fingers and straddled his body. Between her legs, she felt him harden and twitch with anticipation. Despite the revulsion of being with anyone other than Supay, she responded to a sudden surge of desire. Apparently, her siren genetics did not understand monogamy. She would have to push her moral discomfort aside as she pulled Yossele's cock out of his sleeping garment. Like his height and hulking figure suggested, Yossele was more than well endowed. Juno moved her hips until they lined up with his member and slid down. The sudden thickness between her legs caused her to gasp. Beneath her, Yossele was thrusting into her with a rapid, insatiable desire. His sheer strength was leaving bruises on her hips, but she did not care. She moved her hips in time with his and began to orgasm. She threw her head back and started to scream in pleasure before Yossele's hand muffled her cries.

As she orgasmed, Yossele sat up and pulled her legs tighter around his waist. Juno glanced down in surprise realizing he had yet to orgasm. He moaned and thrust deeper inside her; she rocked her hips harder against his. They moved as one in a perfect rhythm that rippled within the stillness of the night. Time ceased to exist for either of them as the act of their passion rose to a crescendo. With a cry of pleasure, Juno began to orgasm around Yossele. His warm semen filled her as he reached climax. While her intense desire faded to a memory, Juno allowed her body to collapse around Yossele. This encounter would not make her task any easier.

Juno ran her fingers along Yossele's arms as she waited for him to become drowsy again. She hated herself intensely for everything that was about to happen. In her mind, she tried to justify her experience with Yossele as the only way out. It most likely was the only way to gain his trust, but she feared it was more than that. In the recesses of her mind, Juno wondered if this is what it meant to be a siren. Would she be consigned to spend her entire life with a desire she was not able not control? Worse, would she have to continually perform such distasteful tasks to remain a part of the siren community? Each time she took a step closer to her mother and towards becoming a full-fledged siren, a piece of her humanity and spirit fell away. Once she was finished, Juno was afraid nothing would be left of the girl she was and the woman she had hoped to be.

Yossele was almost asleep again. With her eyes raised to the heavens, she murmured a prayer to Venus that everything would run smoothly once again. She reached for the piece of paper.

"Yossele," she whispered. "Yossele, darling. Please read this to me?" She held out the piece of paper and she waited.

Still drowsy from sleep, Yossele cracked his eyes to read the paper. "*Ja sam mogę ci rozkazywać, golema,*" he said.

Yossele's eyes widened as the meaning of the words dawned on him. Before him, Juno whispered, "*Ja sam mogę ci rozkazywać, golema.*" She paused, uncertain if the words had worked. "Sit up, Yossele."

Yossele sat upright as commanded. He gulped. "You don't know what you are doing. The more I am commanded, the more likely it is I will lose my mind like the other golems. This is not a good thing." He closed his eyes in pain. How stupid he had been to think this woman was a dream.

Juno took a deep breath. "I can't help it. This is how things must be. Behold." She waved her hand across her abdomen and her mother's spell lifted. For the first time, Yossele saw her growing belly. "This is Supay's child. My mother thinks you are the father. If I don't do something, the child, Supay and I will all be dead. Sirens seldom forgive and their vengeance is total."

Yossele's eyes widened in disbelief. He reached out his hand and rubbed her belly gently. With a heavy heart, he took a deep breath. "I'm familiar with sirens. Your family of daemons is not the group to be crossed. This is my nephew... or niece?" He glanced at her again and waited.

In the darkness, Juno nodded. "Yes, it is. Before I give you the order, I want to ask you if you will help me. I will still force you to carry out the task, but I want to know if you would do this first. I know you just met me, but it is Supay's life and his child's life that also matter."

Yossele took a deep breath and tried to calm his mind. Over the span of a few moments, his entire life had changed. She had not said it yet, but he sensed the end was near. For his brother, he would do anything. They had both been raised by their father together and spent a lifetime trusting each other without question. It was only a matter of time before someone discovered the way to command Yossele. Once that occurred, it would only be a few more years until the constant commands and subservience began to break his mind. At least this way, he would be able to go out in style and save his brother's life. He turned to Juno again and nodded. "Yes, you can. As long as each part of tonight leads to the continued life and happiness of my brother, I will help you."

Juno stood up and threw some clothes at Yossele. "Put these on. Once you are ready, it will be time to go out to the barn. You are to attack Supay and make him fear for his life. He needs to think you have succumbed to the madness of the golem and are beyond hope. No matter what, he is supposed to win the fight and kill you. All this, I command you, golem. Ja sam mogę ci rozkazywać, golema. Do you understand?"

Yossele stumbled while trying to put on his clothes. He nodded at Juno without responding. As if in a dream, he finished dressing and began to walk down the stairs. At the bottom, Juno motioned for him to pause while she grabbed her shoes.

Dashing into a strand of trees downwind from the barn, she peered out in pensive agony. Here was the moment where she would discover if her plan worked. She had to save Supay from her mother's wrath and the potential anger of any siren that discovered them.

Chapter Four

Juno rubbed her belly in an effort to calm her nerves as she waited anxiously from behind the tree. Nothing worked to reassure herself this was the right path. In front of her eyes, Yossele was stumbling out of the house. He had entered the patch of grass in front of the barn and was waiting for Supay. Accustomed to sleeping in his dog form, Supay would soon hear Yossele in front of the barn. All it took was a short wait.

A sudden cracking of twigs caused Juno to jump. Next to her was Circe. Her eyes widened as she glanced over at her mother. How much had Circe been present for? Patting Juno's arm reassuringly, Circe motioned to the barn door. The head of Supay was peeking around the corner. "Stop cowering, Juno. You have arranged the death of your lover, Yossele, in magnificent style. Truly, I am impressed. Few other sirens would be able to pull off such a death without leaving their mark in any way." She glanced coolly over at Juno. Beneath her watchful gaze, Juno straightened her back and tried to watch dispassionately. Next to her, Circe smiled. Her daughter was developing the heart and soul of a real siren. "Well, Juno, I will leave you to enjoy this havoc you have created. We will still need to figure out a solution for the child, but I think we may be able to let it live." Circe patted her on the arm again and disappeared.

Juno sighed in relief. Her secret relationship with Supay was still a secret. Circe must have read the plans she had created and left on her desk. At least this small portion of the day was going as planned.

With her full attention to the scene at hand, Juno winced. Supay had left the barn and approached Yossele in confusion. Without saying anything, Yossele had swung a branch at Supay's figure. Barely jumping away from the swinging branch, Supay transformed into the figure of a wildcat. Circling the ground in front of Yossele, Supay struggled to find a way to calm his brother down. He had expected the madness to arrive someday, but today was not the day he believed it to happen. Distracted for a moment, Supay had to leap to jump free of Yossele's onslaught.

Although Yossele's mind still thought normally, his body was forced to follow Juno's commands. Swinging the branch again, he narrowly missed Supay. 'Idiot,' he thought. When faced with an insane, enraged golem, his brother had chosen to take on an animal form he was unfamiliar with. It was far too late to point this out to Supay now, but Yossele could not help thinking it.

Confused, Supay leapt from rock to rock. It would be impossible to stop his brother. Each swing made Supay realize even more that his brother intended to kill him. Swallowing his fear, Supay continued to avoid Yossele's swings. He had once promised Yossele that he, Supay, would put Yossele out of his misery if this day came. Unfortunately, Supay could not imagine doing such a thing. Unable to follow through on his promise, Supay dodged each attack from the muscular Yossele. Without meaning to, he allowed himself to be hit by the branch. The sudden impact propelled his wild cat body across the field in an instant. Supay's head hit a stray rock which knocked him unconscious as he hit the ground.

From behind the tree, Juno cried out in fear. A sudden pain burst from her womb as she released her cry. Her eyes widened. After discovering the pregnancy, her mother had warned her about labor. It was not supposed to begin yet, but it seemed like the moment was upon her. She groaned in pain. Before she returned to the safety of home, she had to make sure Supay was going to be all right.

On the field, Yossele waited for Supay to wake up. Shrugging, he glanced over at Juno. "He's out. Should I give him a knife or something? This is going to go all night at this rate."

Juno motioned for silence and shook her head. "You," she said, panting, "need to attack with more force. He needs to be convinced that you will kill him." Juno crouched on her knees in agony as she said the last word. Realizing what her whimpers of pain meant, Yossele's eyes widened. This was his last chance to ensure this little family would remain safe.

With his attention back on Supay, he pulled a dagger from his belt. Supay was still not awake, but Yossele could fix that. He yelled out a war cry and descended upon the body of Supay. With the dagger held high above his head, Yossele began to plunge it into Supay's heart. Awoken by the yelling, Supay saw the dagger fall just in time. Using his wild cat reflexes to jump out of the way, he shape shifted into the form of a bear. Without a second thought, he went at the fighting form of Yossele and allowed the bear's nature to take over his mind. Shreds of Yossele flew across the yard as the grizzly bear's mind and soul pushed any feelings from Supay away.

From behind the tree, Juno sank down into a small ball and held her belly. Tears fell from her eyes as the bear —Supay —ran off into the distance. Labor pains wracked her body, but that mattered less than the emotional turmoil she now felt. Supay was gone for the moment, but he was alive. He would never be the innocent young man or sweet lover she had known, but he would live. She glanced out across the field and stumbled to her feet. Someday, Supay would be with someone else and he would be happy. It was worth it. The emotional decision that had taken such a toll on her soul would be worth it if Supay and her child remained alive. She clenched her belly in agony and stumbled upon the path home.

-To be continued in Book 8-

If you enjoyed this title, I would appreciate your leaving a review of the book. Good reviews encourage an author to write as well as help books to sell. Good reviews can be just a few short sentences describing

what you liked about the book without having a spoiler.
If you could spend 30 seconds writing a review, I
would appreciate it: you can review this title right now
at your favorite retailer.

Here is a preview of the **next story** you may enjoy:

Duplicity - The Daemon Paranormal Romance Chronicles, Book 8

IT HAD been several months since the trauma around Supay and Yossele had died down. From that time on, Juno had carefully avoided seeing Supay. She spent most of her days at home with her new-born daughter, Maia. Wrapped up in the joys of motherhood, she had managed to put the tragic events out of her mind temporarily.

Turning a corner, Juno sighed in relief. Circe must be out for the day. Soon enough, Juno's training ought to begin. Hopefully, she would be able to spend more time with her daughter before that happened. Upon hearing the gurgles and giggles of Maia, Juno returned to the nursery. She picked her daughter up, sat down on a rocking chair in the room and began to play with her.

"You look just like daddy," she cooed as she tickled Maia under the chin. Her gentle tickles were rewarded with a beautiful smile. "We'll see him someday, my love. We just have to wait for the right time." Juno held her daughter closer and started to rock gently back and forth. Before long, the motion would help Maia return to dreamland. Sighing in happiness, she relaxed for a few moments. Without Circe here, she could stop being so tense.

Juno set her daughter back into the crib and tiptoed quietly out of the room. Turning around, she ran into Circe. Juno smiled pleasantly as she tried to hide her surprise. "I did not expect to see you here, Mother. How has your day been?" she asked.

Circe motioned for her to follow her to the kitchen. "My dear, I am afraid that it is time for you to finish your training. I have just the dress in mind."

Confused, Juno followed her into the kitchen. On the table, a button-up black dress was carefully laid out with matching heels. She looked at Circe inquisitively. "What do you mean… *finish my training?*"

Shaking her head, Circe handed Juno the shoes to try on. "It is not quite over with. A siren's training is unique to each siren. Since you reached adulthood a year ago, I had waited patiently for you to take your first lover. Like every young siren, you were unable to control yourself and soon were with child. Your actual training started on the night that you had to end the affair. Sirens do not love. We manipulate and we wreak havoc on the humans around us. Your first test was to do so with the man that you loved. I had thought at the time that you had done an admirably good job. Unlike many young sirens, you were able to manage the matter without leaving your fingerprints upon the results."

Circe sat down and crossed her legs delicately. "Unfortunately, my suspicion about the parentage of your child was confirmed by what I just heard in the nursery. You still have to end things with Supay. If you are able to ruin your relationship well enough for him to never return, I will allow your daughter to live."

Juno's eyes flashed angrily and fear crept into her mind. She consciously tried to control her thoughts. Somehow, she had to get free of the siren world. She would never be able to love who she wished or raise her daughter if sirens were involved. For the moment, her primary focus would be to ensure the safety of her child. "What will happen to Maia if I do this?" she asked in a cold monotone. Never again would Juno let Circe realize her pain.

If you enjoyed this sample then look for **Duplicity - The Daemon Paranormal Romance Chronicles, Book 8**.

Here is a preview of **another story** you may enjoy:

Evil Lust - The Leather Satchel Paranormal Romance Series, Book 3

VALTINA WAITED patiently for Ladaya to return with her next assignment. She didn't know how much time had passed since she last saw her mentor. Time ran differently in Middle World, much more slowly than on Earth or in The Afterlife. Valtina had stopped trying to keep up with it several lifetimes ago, but Ladaya's absence seemed long, even by Middle World standards.

As she waited, Valtina wondered where Ladaya would send her next. She was determined to earn her way into The Afterlife, and she was full of confidence that she would be successful. Her recent mission had been challenging but rewarding… Amy and Kyle were meant to be together. Matt was a lost cause and Valtina was able to finesse the situation for the best outcome. In just two days, she was able to create a long-lasting relationship that should have happened a lot sooner. Valtina was certain she could handle any assignment Ladaya gave her.

The last assignment was actually enjoyable. In fact, Valtina would probably have accepted the mission even if Ladaya hadn't offered The Afterlife as a reward. In each of her lives, Valtina had been a passionate, sexual person. She'd never enjoyed sex just for the sake of sex. In each life she'd found her soul-mate, the one person whose spirit understood hers. And in each life, she and her soul-mate had enjoyed passionate, adventurous sex.

"I guess I am uniquely qualified for this job," Valtina thought out loud.

"You certainly are," said a familiar voice behind her. Valtina turned and found Ladaya approaching. She looked tired… and a little worried.

"Are you alright?" Valtina asked.

"It's been a long three days." Ladaya sighed. "We're losing ground. We've tapped every resource we have, but evil is still winning. Their numbers are multiplying as ours dwindle. There's still hope, of course, I just never thought it would get this far." Ladaya smiled sadly.

"What can I do, Ladaya?" Valtina asked determinedly.

"We're fighting many dark forces," Ladaya explained, "forces that for centuries were happy to fight amongst themselves. Humans have always been affected by them, but never to such a large scale. But a few decades ago, these forces decided to unite under a common goal. Since then, their sole focus has been to end existence as we know it. And, as you know, the only way to do that is to rid the world of love. If the last drop of love dies, every living organism will follow… the barren earth will be left to every foul creature that's ever been created. I'm sorry if this sounds repetitive, Valtina, but you MUST understand the importance of your missions."

"I understand, Ladaya. Just tell me where to go next."

"This case is much different than your last mission," Ladaya began. "Claire and Henry are married, and they're meant to be. But there are forces working against them… powerful forces. In fact, Valtina, I'm about to put you up against, essentially, your evil twin."

"My evil twin? I'm afraid I'm going to need you to explain that," Valtina said, taken aback.

"Think Valtina. Your strength, your love, your goodness, they're all rooted in your sexuality. What's the evil counterpart to that?"

Valtina thought for a moment, and then gasped. "You can't be serious," she said firmly. "They don't exist. Not anymore."

"That's what we thought, but we were wrong. I think they've been waiting… the other creatures have set everything up just right, and now they've come out of hiding and they're moving in for the final play."

"So… you're sending me after…"

"Yes. A succubus," Ladaya interrupted. "I'm not sure of her true name, but Henry knows her as Charlotte. It's important that we move quickly. Henry has only been under her spell for a few days. Claire and Henry have a nine-month-old baby, so Claire is distracted and hasn't noticed any change in her husband. If we can keep her from finding out, we can save their marriage. We could wipe her memory, but we can't erase the scars left by that deep of a betrayal. If she learns of Henry's infidelity, their love will die."

"We won't let evil win Ladaya, I'll do my best work." Valtina took her friend by the hand and met her eyes. "My absolute best work. I promise."

"You must Valtina." She sighed, squeezing her hand. "Once you've broken the spell Charlotte has on Henry, wipe his memory of her. He isn't cheating on purpose… she has total control. This isn't something he should suffer for."

"But how do I break the spell?" Valtina asked.

"Follow your instincts," Ladaya smiled. "This is one area in which they've always served you well. Now, you'd probably be able to spot the succubus anyway, but your new powers will allow you to see her true form. You'll see the true form of other creatures as well. Do NOT react when you see them. Some monsters can see spirits, so you don't want to draw attention to yourself. If you're ever in true danger I'll sense it, and I'll send help immediately."

Valtina wasn't scared. As a matter of fact, this was the most exhilarated she'd felt since she entered Middle World. Once again, she had a purpose, a reason for being. "What do you want me to do with the succubus after I've broken her spell?" she asked fiercely.

"Nothing," Ladaya responded firmly. "You are to focus on your mission, and your mission alone. We have others in our ranks who are equipped to fight monsters. But the connection between her and Henry must be broken first, or anything we do to her will happen to him too."

"I'll do it as quickly as possible," Valtina promised. "I'll see you soon." She smiled at Ladaya as the fog surrounded her, transporting her to Henry and Claire's bedroom.

If you enjoyed this sample then look for **Evil Lust - The Leather Satchel Paranormal Romance Series, Book 3**.

Other Books by Darla Dunbar

- The Romeo Alpha BBW Paranormal Shifter Romance Series

- Romeo Alpha Blood Lines Romance

- The Alpha Feud BBW Paranormal Shifter Romance Series

- The Alpha Packed BBW Paranormal Shifter Romance Series

- The Mind Talker Paranormal Romance Series

- The Leather Satchel Paranormal Romance Series

Get the latest update on new releases from the author at:

https://darladunbar.com/newsletter/

About the Author - Darla Dunbar

Darla has been interested in paranormal romance since she was a teenager in high school. It was then that she discovered she could fulfill her fantasies through her writing.

Observing people and human behavior in the area of romance has always been one of her favorite pastimes. Combining that with an overactive imagination is a sure fire way of coming up with interesting themes.

Connect with Darla Dunbar

I really appreciate you reading my book! Here are my social media coordinates:

Friend me on Facebook:
https://www.facebook.com/darladunbar/

Follow me on Twitter: https://twitter.com/DarlDunbar

Check me out on Goodreads:
https://www.goodreads.com/author/show/8425857.Darl
a_Dunbar

Subscribe to my newsletter:
https://darladunbar.com/newsletter/

Visit my website: https://darladunbar.com/